The Sheep Beauty

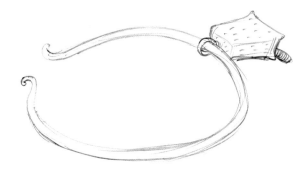

This book is edited and designed by the Editorial Committee of *Cultural China* series

Story and Illustrations: Li Jian
Translation: Yijin Wert

Editorial Assistant: Logan Louis
Editor: Yang Xiaohe
Editorial Director: Zhang Yicong

Senior Consultants: Sun Yong, Wu Ying, Yang Xinci
Managing Director and Publisher: Wang Youbu

ISBN: 978-1-60220-988-6

Address any comments about *Stories of the Chinese Zodiac: The Sheep Beauty* to:

Better Link Press
99 Park Ave
New York, NY 10016
USA

or

Shanghai Press and Publishing Development Company
F 7 Donghu Road, Shanghai, China (200031)
Email: comments_betterlinkpress@hotmail.com

Printed in China by Shenzhen Donnelley Printing Co., Ltd.

1   3   5   7   9   10   8   6   4   2

羊姑娘
The Sheep Beauty

A Story in English and Chinese

by Li Jian
Translated by Yijin Wert

Better Link Press

There is a small beautiful place called the Sheep Horn Village in China. In the village, there stands a precious rock with a beautiful legend.

在中国，有一个秀丽的地方叫羊角村。村子里，有一块珍贵的石头，它有着美丽的传说。

A long time ago, there lived a highly respected doctor in the village. One day, on his way back home from work, he saw an injured sheep lying on the side of the road. The kind doctor bandaged its wound and took it home.

很久很久以前，村里住着一位医术高明的郎中。一天，他在出诊回家的路上，看见一头受伤的羊躺在路边。心地善良的郎中为羊包扎了伤口，并带它一起回了家。

Every day, when the doctor and his family were changing its bandages, they could hear the sheep "Baa" at them as if it was saying thank you.

The sheep had a speedy recovery after receiving good care from the doctor and his family.

每天，当郎中一家给羊换药时，总见它朝他们"咩咩"地叫，好像在说谢谢。

有了郎中一家人的悉心照料，羊很快恢复了健康。

One day, while the doctor was making plans to return the sheep to its home, he heard a loud ferocious roar.

There came a huge monster who stood at the entrance of the village demanding that each family should offer him a child. If the villagers didn't obey, he would destroy the village before sundown.

一天，郎中正打算将羊送回它自己的家，突然听到了一声凶猛的巨吼。

村口来了一只怪兽，吼叫着要每家送一个小孩子给他。如果村民们不照办，他就会在太阳落山前毁掉村子。

The villagers were so scared that they didn't know how to deal with the monster. They gathered at the doctor's house to seek a solution.

村民们都很害怕，不知道该怎么办才好。他们聚到郎中家里想办法。

It was almost sundown. The doctor was very nervous pacing up and down with his child in his arms. Seeing him in great fear, the sheep suddenly opened its mouth, "My dear savior, let me help you!" This took the villagers by surprise. "What's your plan?" asked the doctor.

眼看太阳就要落山了，郎中焦急地抱着自己的孩子走来走去。羊看见他这么害怕，突然开口说话了："恩人，让我来帮助你们吧！"村民们吃惊极了。郎中问："你有什么办法呢？"

The villagers were stunned when they saw the sheep rolling itself over the floor and transforming itself to a beautiful young girl.

"Wait for my good news at home," the Sheep Beauty rushed out of the door as she spoke.

羊在地上打了一个滚，竟变成了一个漂亮的小姑娘！村民们更吃惊了。
"你们就在家等我的好消息吧！"羊姑娘说完就出门了。

At the entrance of the village, the Sheep Beauty saw the monster walking into the village. She ran to the monster and acted very nervously. "Bad news! There came another monster who also demanded a child from each family. Please go and drive him away, otherwise you will not get any child," the Sheep Beauty said.

羊姑娘来到村口，看见怪兽正朝村子里走来。她赶紧跑过去，假装很着急。"不好了！村外边又来了一只怪兽，也要每家送一个小孩子给它。你快去把他赶跑吧，要不然就没有小孩子送给你了。"

"What? Where is he? Take me there!" the monster yelled furiously. The Sheep Beauty immediately took him to look for the other monster.

"什么，他在哪？快带我去找他！"怪兽气得大叫。羊姑娘赶紧领着他去找另外一只怪兽。

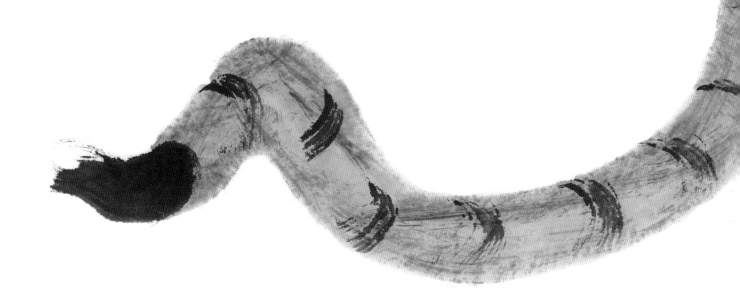

The Sheep Beauty took the monster away from the village. They walked over the muddy land …

羊姑娘领着怪兽远离了村子。他们走过泥地……

And crossed over the mountains and valleys …

穿过山谷……

And passed through the spring …

绕过山泉……

After they circled around for a long time, they came to the muddy land again. The monster got mad because he couldn't find the other monster. The Sheep Beauty pointed to the footprints on the mud and said, "Look! These are the footprints of the other monster. It looks like he was heading towards the mountains."

The monster looked down at the footprints and immediately rushed towards the mountains by following the footprints.

用了好长时间转了一大圈，他们又回到了泥地里。还是找不到另一只怪兽，怪兽很生气。羊姑娘指着泥地里的脚印说："看，这些是那怪兽的脚印，他好像是朝山里去了！"

怪兽低头一看，立刻跟着地上的脚印往山里跑。

The monster screamed as he ran. "Where are you, Monster? Don't you dare to come out!" Suddenly the mountains were echoed with the same screaming, "Where are you, Monster? Don't you dare to come out!"

怪兽边跑边吼："怪兽，你在哪？敢不敢出来！"谁知，山谷里传来了一模一样的怒吼，"怪兽，你在哪？敢不敢出来！"

The monster got even more irritated. "It seems that the sound came from over there," the Sheep Beauty said as she was pointing towards the spring. The monster came to the spring where he found a monster looking at him in the water.

As the monster showed his sharp teeth, he saw the monster in the water also showing his sharp teeth. As the monster was waving his sharp claws, he saw the monster in the water also waving his sharp claws …

怪兽更恼怒了。羊姑娘指着山泉那边说:"声音好像从那边传来的!"怪兽跑到泉水边一看,水里果然有一只怪兽正盯着自己。

怪兽露出尖尖的牙齿,水里的怪兽也露出尖尖的牙齿;他舞动锋利的爪子,水里的怪兽也舞动锋利的爪子……

This made the monster go totally crazy that he jumped into the water,
attempting to catch the other monster.

The Sheep Beauty heard a big splashing sound. The monster fell into the
water and was washed away by the rough currents of the spring.

怪兽彻底被激怒了，一下子跳起来扑向水里那个讨厌鬼。

羊姑娘听到"扑通"一声，怪兽掉进了水里，被湍急的溪流冲走了。

The Sheep Beauty delivered the good news to the villagers when she returned to the doctor's home. Since the monster was driven away, she decided to leave too.

The villagers begged her to stay, but the Sheep Beauty refused. She transformed herself back to a sheep and left the village.

羊姑娘回到郎中家，告诉了大家这个好消息。既然怪兽已经被赶跑了，她自己也要走了。

村民们再三挽留她留下，但羊姑娘拒绝了。她还是变回了羊，离开了村子。

As the monster realized that he was fooled by the Sheep Beauty, he crawled out of the spring and returned to the village. He tried to kill the first person he saw …

当怪兽意识到自己上了羊姑娘的当，他爬上了岸，回到了村子。他向进村后看见的第一个人扑过去……

Just at that moment, the sheep dashed over and blocked the monster. As the monster ran into the sheep, they both turned into rock.

The villagers were greatly touched by the Sheep Beauty's sacrifice. To commemorate her, they named their village "Sheep Horn". The precious rock is still in the village today.

正在这时，羊冲了出来，挡住了怪兽。怪兽冲撞到羊的瞬间，他们一起变成了石头。

村民们很感激羊姑娘。为了纪念她，把这个山村改名叫"羊角村"。现在，这块宝贵的石头还在村子里呢。

Lunar Years of the Sheep in the Western Calendar

5 Feb 1919–4 Feb 1920	5 Feb 1931–4 Feb 1932	5 Feb 1943–4 Feb 1944
4 Feb 1955–4 Feb 1956	4 Feb 1967–4 Feb 1968	4 Feb 1979–4 Feb 1980
4 Feb 1991–3 Feb 1992	4 Feb 2003–3 Feb 2004	4 Feb 2015–3 Feb 2016
4 Feb 2027–3 Feb 2028	4 Feb 2039–3 Feb 2040	4 Feb 2051–3 Feb 2052

The Docile and Compassionate Sheep

The eighth sign of the Chinese zodiac symbolizes obedience and kindness. People born in the year of the Sheep are sensitive, prudent and upright. Beneath the Sheep's mild exterior lies an inner strength. They are able to protect themselves when needed. They are selfless and easily touched by the misfortune of others.

The Sheep can seem pessimistic and be a worrier. They tend to resign themselves to fate and don't like to be stuck with routines.

温顺善良的羊

羊在十二生肖中排第八，代表着温顺和善良。属羊的人多愁善感，深谋远虑，正直诚实，外表温柔但内心坚持己见，自我保护意识很强。他们无私忘我，易被别人的不幸经历所感染。

属羊的人有时悲观、忧虑，喜欢听天由命，不喜欢日常的例行工作。